Lost in
New York

CATCH FLAT STANLEY'S WORLDWIDE ADVENTURES:

FLAT STANLEY'S

WORLDWIDE ADVENTURES

BOOK No. 15

Lost in
New York

CREATED BY **Jeff Brown**
WRITTEN BY **Kate Egan**
PICTURES BY **Macky Pamintuan**

HARPER
An Imprint of HarperCollinsPublishers

Flat Stanley's Worldwide Adventures #15: Lost in New York
Text copyright © 2018 by the Trust u/w/o Richard Brown f/b/o Duncan Brown
Illustrations © 2018 by Macky Pamintuan
www.harpercollinschildrens.com
Library of Congress Control Number: 2018938252
ISBN 978-0-06-236610-8 (trade bdg.)—ISBN 978-0-06-236609-2 (pbk.)
Typography by Alison Klapthor
18 19 20 21 22   CG/LSCC   10 9 8 7 6 5 4 3 2 1
❖
First Edition

CONTENTS

The Crown of New York

Stanley Lambchop was climbing stairs.

His legs were getting wobbly, and his breath was getting heavy, but he couldn't stop now. He was determined to get to the top!

Stanley turned to look behind him. A long spiral staircase twisted down to the ground floor.

He turned to look above him. The

rest of the spiral staircase stretched as far as his eyes could see.

"Are we almost there?" Stanley said to his mother, who was a few steps in front of him. But she couldn't even hear him. There was a crowd of people ahead of Mrs. Lambchop, and another crowd of people behind Stanley. Metal walls wrapped around the busy staircase, and voices echoed everywhere.

Stanley counted the steps. "One hundred and twenty-one. One hundred and twenty-two," he said. He knew there were 354 steps altogether, so he still had a long way to go. By the time he got to 210, Stanley needed a break.

Luckily, he had a special superpower

that would allow him to rest in the middle of this crowd. Some time ago, a bulletin board had fallen off his bedroom wall and left him as flat as a pancake. Since he didn't take up much space, he could stop on the stairs without bothering anyone!

Stanley flattened himself against the cool metal wall and took a gulp of air. The people kept rushing past him. In a minute, he felt rested and ready to climb again. There was only one problem! He'd lost Mrs. Lambchop.

Stanley peeled himself off the wall and tried to catch a glimpse of her.

"Mom!" Stanley called. But she still

couldn't hear him in all the noise.

Stanley took another deep breath. He knew what to do if he got lost. His mother must have talked him through it a hundred times. "Stay calm," Stanley told himself. "That is the first step. Then ask for help if you need it."

He looked at the people all around him. How would he know who to ask?

Then he realized something. The staircase traffic was only going one way. If he kept on climbing, his mother would be waiting at the top.

"Two hundred and fifteen," Stanley counted. "Two hundred and sixteen."

Finally, the stairs ended in a domed

room with a long row of windows.

"There you are!" said Mrs. Lambchop. "I was starting to get a little worried."

"Come and see!" yelled Stanley's younger brother, Arthur. He was standing at a window with their father, holding a camera.

From the window, Stanley could see a city skyline, with more skyscrapers than he could ever count. Between him and the city there was a sparkling river crisscrossed by bridges. Stanley saw boats bobbing in the water, and planes speeding toward a nearby airport. It was a great view of a very busy place!

Then he craned his neck to see what

was directly beneath him.

He saw a huge, mint-green hand holding a book.

And above him, seven spikes of a crown, casting shadows on the water below.

Stanley and his family were standing inside the crown of the Statue of Liberty! From where they stood, they could see all of New York City.

This was the first stop on the Lambchops' first trip to New York. Stanley had been invited to a special gathering of children from all over the world. They would be meeting at a famous place called the United Nations to sign a Declaration of Friendship—a promise to be a good friend to the whole world.

Stanley Lambchop was an experienced traveler. He had already been to many countries. Now he would be able to meet kids from some of the places he had not yet visited. Stanley couldn't wait.

But first he was seeing some of New York's most famous sights with his family.

Arthur snapped pictures from each of the twenty-five windows in the statue's crown. Then he turned to Stanley and said, "This is a great view of the city. But you know the one thing we can't see?"

"What's that?" Stanley asked.

"The Statue of Liberty!" said Arthur.

That is strange but true, Stanley thought. Here inside the statue, they were too close to see what it really looked like. From the window, he could see the folds in the statue's robes, and a bird sitting on one of its fingers! But for the complete

view, he would have to wait until they got back onto the ferry that took people to and from Liberty Island. "I get the camera on the ride back," he reminded his brother.

Stanley walked over to where a sign explained a bit about the statue's history. "Dedicated in 1886, the statue was a gift from the people of France to the people of the United States," Stanley read out loud. "Today, she represents freedom and liberty around the world."

Mrs. Lambchop nudged him. "That is why the book she holds has 'July fourth' written on the cover," she explained. "The Fourth of July was the day our country broke free from England."

She led both boys to a window and pointed at another island down below. "Do you know what that is?" she asked.

Arthur shrugged. "No idea," he admitted.

"That is Ellis Island," said Mrs. Lambchop. "For many years, newcomers to the United States stopped there before they could enter the country. Many of them were looking for freedom they did not have at home. From there, they could see the Statue of Liberty. She reminded them of what they would find in America."

"Newcomers?" Stanley asked.

"People who were moving to America from places all over the world," Mrs.

Lambchop explained. "They hoped they would have a better life here."

"Well . . . did they?" asked Arthur.

"Yes, they did," said Mrs. Lambchop, smiling. "Now New York is home to people from all around the globe."

Stanley nodded his head. "That is pretty cool," he said. "People from around the world come to live in New York. And people from around the world come to meet at the United Nations!"

"That *is* cool," Arthur agreed. "And that reminds me of something. Are you ready for the gift shop?"

Stanley nodded again and they all started for the stairs. Walking down the spiral staircase was almost harder than climbing up! By the time he reached the bottom, Stanley's legs were like jelly. But he had an important job to do at the gift shop.

All the children gathering at the United Nations needed to bring an item from their home country to show to the others. It would be like show-and-tell from around the world! Stanley had already decided to bring a souvenir from the Statue of Liberty. What could be more American than that?

The only problem was that Stanley did not know what to choose. The gift shop had T-shirts and baseball caps that said "I heart New York." It had key

chains and bookmarks and magnets.
That won't work, Stanley thought. You
can get a magnet anywhere!

He picked up a tiny replica of the
Statue of Liberty, all in gold. Too bad
it cost forty dollars! He wound up
a music box that played "The Star-
Spangled Banner."

He was almost ready to give up when
he saw it. His very own
Statue of Liberty
crown! Stanley
did not like
wearing hats,
because they
flopped over
his flat head.

But this crown fit like a headband. It was easy to carry, because it was made of foam, and it did not cost too much. It would remind him of where he had just been standing, too. The crown was perfect!

Now everyone at the United Nations will know where I'm from, Stanley thought. A place where people from around the world come together.

Welcome to the UN

Soon after the family woke up the next morning, Mr. Lambchop made a mistake.

Inside their hotel room, he pointed to a map. "We are right here," he said to Stanley. "Eighth Avenue. It should not take too long to get to the United Nations. It is on First Avenue. Just seven streets away from where we are staying."

But as they started their walk for the UN, it turned out there was a lot of distance between the streets. And there were more than seven of them! There were streets that Mr. Lambchop had not even counted, like Madison, Park, and Lexington Avenues. It was lucky they had allowed some extra time for this walk. New York was a huge city! Stanley's legs were getting tired again.

"Can we take a taxi?" Arthur whined.

Stanley liked the sound of that. He knew just how to do it, too. He had seen it in a lot of New York movies! Stanley put his arm in the air and yelled,

"Taxi!" at a yellow cab speeding by.

The taxi did not stop, though. "It already has a passenger," Mrs. Lambchop explained. "Let's keep walking. It won't take much longer now."

Stanley looked up as he walked. The skyscrapers were so high he couldn't see their roofs! The buildings blocked out a lot of light, so the sidewalks below were always in shadow. It was his turn to use the camera, but it was hard to get a good picture.

Whenever the Lambchops crossed an avenue, there was a huge gust of wind. Flat Stanley held his mother's elbow to steady himself. He did not want to blow away into New York's city streets! They were crowded with cars, buses, trucks, bikes, and motorcycles. It sounded like all of them were honking their horns at the same time.

At the next corner, Stanley saw a tall

building that looked like it was made of glass. Next to it was a lower building with a dome. And in front of the domed building, there was a long row of flagpoles. There was a flag for every country that was a part of the United Nations. They had arrived at last!

"Here we are!" said Mr. Lambchop.

Arthur walked along the row of flags, pointing out the ones he knew. "Egypt, Japan, Canada, Mexico, China . . ." Together, they made a rainbow of colors and patterns.

Stanley took a lot of pictures! He was excited to see the flags, but even more excited about meeting the children from around the world. Stanley was always ready to make new friends.

When the Lambchops arrived at the visitors' center, a guide stepped forward to greet them. She had a smart suit on, and her hair was so blonde that it was almost white. "You must be the Lambchop family," she said,

recognizing Stanley. "Welcome to the United Nations—or the UN, as we call it around here. My name is Anya Petersen."

Anya led the family through the visitors' entrance. She opened a door and made a surprising announcement. "Once you walk through this door," she said, "you are no longer in the United States. This building, and the land beneath it, belongs to every country that is part of the UN."

"Look," Arthur said, keeping one foot outside and one foot inside the doorway. "I'm only halfway in America!" he said. Stanley smiled.

"Come along," said Anya. "The other

families are gathered already. Now that you've arrived, we can begin."

Arthur jumped in the air, and his feet left the ground. "Now I'm not in any country at all!" he said. "At least until I land."

The Lambchops followed Anya into a long hallway, where they caught their first glimpse of the other kids and their families. Many of them looked like people Stanley knew from home, wearing jeans and sneakers. But some of the boys were wearing long shirts that looked like tunics. One of the girls had a colorful scarf wrapped around her head.

Stanley wondered where they came from. He wondered what sports they played, what food they ate, what pets they had, what holidays they celebrated. He couldn't wait to talk to them!

But Anya Petersen was talking first.

"Now that we are all here," she said, "I'd like to introduce you to the UN. People come together here from different countries to solve problems peacefully. It is a good place to cooperate on matters that affect us all, like keeping the planet's air and water safe, or making sure that people stay healthy around the world. Usually the people who make these agreements are adults. At this gathering, though, we will be doing something different. Can anyone tell me what it is?"

A boy with bright red hair waved his hand in the air eagerly. "I can! I can!" he said. "We will be making a promise!"

"Yes, that's true," Anya replied. "But a promise to do what?"

A grown-up spoke next. "It's a promise for the next generation," he said.

"For us kids!" a kid shouted. "It's a promise that we will stick together."

A girl next to Stanley raised her hand. Her voice was soft but sure as she explained. "It's a promise that all the children of the world will be friends. If we make that promise now, we can keep the world peaceful even when we're older."

Anya nodded. "That's exactly what a Declaration of Friendship is," she said. "Now, let me show you where we will do the signing."

Anya led the group down a hallway and into a large auditorium. It was much nicer than a school auditorium, though, with bright lights, rows of seats behind gleaming wooden tables, and a circular stage up front. The families filed into the rows of seats and sat down.

As Stanley took his seat, he realized something. No one was really noticing him.

Sometimes people asked him a lot

of questions about his flatness. At the UN, though, Stanley didn't stand out as much. Since there were lots of different kinds of people, he could almost blend into the crowd.

Stanley smiled to himself. It would be easy to make friends here. He would start with the person sitting next to him! It turned out to be the

Noodles for Lunch

Lunch at the UN was not at all like lunch in school. The Lambchops sat at a round table with a crisp white tablecloth and fresh flowers in the middle. They sat with other families from across the globe, who were all wearing name tags. Sometimes they spoke in English, and sometimes they spoke in other languages. But everyone had one thing in common: They were hungry.

For some reason, there were two forks next to Stanley's plate. He handed one of them to the boy from Scotland, who was also at his table. Now Stanley knew that the boy's name was Ian—it was written on his name tag.

"I think I got your fork by mistake," Stanley said.

Ian shook his head. "I don't think

so," he said. "I have two forks, too!"

"Each one is for a different part of the meal," said Mr. Lambchop. "The big one is for the main course, and the small one is for dessert."

"I'm going to use the big one for dessert!" said Arthur. "That way I will get extra!"

"We need to respect the rules here," Mrs. Lambchop reminded Arthur.

"After all, we are the guests."

The rules at the UN were tricky, though, as Stanley was about to find out.

At first, Stanley was excited when bowls of noodles arrived at the tables. Noodles were one of his favorite foods!

But Stanley was used to noodles on a plate, and these noodles were in a bowl of soup. They were long and slippery, and they were hard to eat. Stanley's stomach was rumbling, but he did not know how to get started. He couldn't even catch a noodle with his spoon!

At least he was not the only one having trouble. He looked over at Ian and saw that his noodles were all tangled together. When Ian tried to cut them with a fork and knife, most of his soup ended up on the table.

Luckily, some experts were ready to help.

Marco, from Italy, said "Looks like you are having a hard time! Let me show you another way." He stabbed his fork into the middle of his bowl, and twirled. He kept twirling until the noodles were wrapped around the fork in a clump that was just the right size to pop into his mouth. "Mmm! Delicious!" he said.

Stanley had tried this in the past, but never got it right. He tried to copy Marco, but his clump of noodles was so big that he had to start all over twice. They were starting to get a little cold.

"We love noodles in Thailand," said a girl named Kamala. She used a pair of chopsticks to pick up one noodle. She pinched the noodle firmly and held on tight. She had no trouble eating it at all.

Stanley had not noticed he had chopsticks alongside his two forks. He tried to balance them between his fingers, like Kamala did. But he could not grasp a noodle. He could not even grasp the piece of carrot that was floating in his soup.

"It takes a lot of

practice," Kamala said kindly.

Marco and Kamala were both super nice, but Stanley was still stuck.

"Look! I think I've got it!" Ian had a noodle trapped between two chopsticks. He bent down low so his mouth was just above the bowl. He tipped his head back and dropped the noodle in. He peered into his bowl and counted. "One down, twenty more to go."

Marco and his family had finished their noodles already. Stanley's mother was wiping her mouth with a napkin. It's now or never! Stanley thought. Pretty soon, someone would come to take the noodles away.

Stanley put down the chopsticks and

tried one more time with his spoon.

This time, he handled the noodle just right. It started slipping only when Stanley lifted the spoon to his lips. And Stanley was not going to let this noodle get away! Loudly, he slurped it up and swallowed.

"Stanley!" said Mrs. Lambchop. "Please don't slurp! Watch your manners!"

Stanley turned bright red. He had not meant to be rude. He did not want to miss his last chance with the first noodle.

But Meera, from India, stepped in to save him. "In some countries, slurping is considered polite," she pointed out.

"It's not bad manners at all. It's the way you tell the cook you enjoyed the meal."

Stanley smiled, glad to hear that. But now he did not know what to do. Which set of noodle-eating rules should he follow? His mother's, or Marco's, or Kamala's, or Meera's? Everyone had a different way! Stanley really wanted to do what Ian did, which was to pick up the whole bowl and drink it, but he had a feeling his mother wouldn't like that, either.

Before he could make up his mind, Anya Petersen called for everyone's attention.

"While we wait for our next course," she announced, "we will share the

41

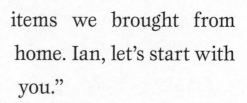

items we brought from home. Ian, let's start with you."

Ian stood proudly and held up a plaid skirt. "This is called a kilt. People in Scotland wear these on special occasions," he explained. "Even the boys!" He pointed out the red-and-blue plaid pattern of the cloth. "Many families have a special pattern for their kilts," he said. "The patterns are passed down to children and grandchildren."

Everyone at the table smiled and nodded. Meera stood up next. She had brought a tiny model of a famous

And if you climb all the way up the spiral staircase—inside the statue—you will be able to go to the crown and see the New York City skyline across the river!"

"After lunch," said Anya, "we will begin our New York City tour. I can help anyone who might like to see the Statue of Liberty. Now, who would like to share next?"

After Stanley showed his crown, a few other kids showed items that Stanley had seen before. That was because the items were not special to any one country—they were just things that the kids who brought them cared about, like stuffed animals, toy cars, and action figures. "Hey, I have the same Super Looper game!" Arthur called out when a boy from South Africa showed everyone his favorite toy.

Some things were the same no matter where you were from, Stanley figured.

Even if you ate noodles in a completely different way.

Train Stations

The New York City tour would begin at a train station. Grand Central Terminal was a short walk from the UN, and from there the group would take the famous New York City subway to see some other sights.

"Grand Central is one of New York's landmarks," said Anya as she opened the door for all of them to walk through.

"It is one of the largest train stations in the world. It is also one of the most spectacular!"

Stanley saw what she meant when he stepped inside. Grand Central Terminal was so huge that he guessed a whole train could fit in it! It was full of people in a rush, carrying bags and checking the time. There were shops and restaurants for them to enjoy, but no one seemed to be stopping.

Anya said, "Here at Grand Central, you can see why some people call New York 'the city that never sleeps.'"

Stanley worried about getting crushed in the rush. But he also liked that no one was staring at him. The

New Yorkers had other things to do!

Anya led the group into a quiet spot near an information booth. "As we walk to the subway, be sure to look at the ceiling," she told them.

Stanley looked up, and he couldn't believe it! The ceiling of Grand Central Terminal was painted pale blue, with gold stars. It looked like the night sky, with all the constellations out at once. He nudged his brother. "I need the camera right away!" he said. "I have to get some pictures of this!"

Ian was standing right next to Stanley. He said "Look, there's the Big Dipper! Make sure you get a picture of that!"

Stanley snapped pictures of the ceiling from every angle. He got the Big Dipper, the Little Dipper, and Orion's Belt.

"Now get a picture of me!" Ian insisted.

He stood in front of Stanley's camera, blocking the ceiling completely. All Stanley could see was Ian, sticking out his tongue.

"Look at this!" said Ian after Stanley put the camera down. He held his nose and shimmied toward the floor, pretending he had just jumped into a pool of water. Ian was pretty funny! Stanley could not stop laughing.

"Stick with us, boys," said Mrs.

Lambchop. The group was walking away, so Stanley and Ian hurried to catch up. They went down a long ramp and pushed through a turnstile. Then, suddenly, they were on a narrow subway platform!

It was deep beneath the main floor of Grand Central Terminal, with no sunlight and a damp smell.

Ian whispered, "I hear that sometimes there are rats on the subway tracks."

Stanley shuddered. But all he could see on the tracks were some pieces of trash.

The group from the UN spread out along the platform. Anya spoke loudly

to explain what they were doing next,
her voice bouncing and echoing against
the tiled wall.

"We will be taking a train to Times

Square," she said. "From there, we will continue on to the Empire State Building. As we move about the city, I ask that you keep some safety tips in mind. New York is a big place, so we will want to stick together. Make sure that valuables like wallets are tucked away. Try to avoid talking to strangers."

After she finished with these precautions, Anya promised that their train would be there any minute.

Many minutes passed, though, and it still hadn't come.

"When will it get here?" Ian asked Stanley.

"When will it get here?" Stanley asked his mother.

"I don't know," said Mrs. Lambchop. "But there are ways to tell when the train is approaching. First you will hear a rumbling in the distance. Then you will see a light in that long tunnel."

Stanley leaned toward the edge of the subway platform and craned his neck to see. There was no light yet. Where the platform ended, the train tracks just continued into darkness.

Ian leaned so far that Mrs. Lambchop had to pull him back! While Ian's parents were chatting with another family, Mrs. Lambchop was looking out for him.

She pointed out a yellow stripe on the platform. "Let's make sure to stand behind the line," she told both boys. "That way, you will stay safe when the train arrives."

Stanley slumped onto a bench. He was tired of waiting.

He still couldn't hear or see a train coming. But he heard something else. "Ian! Do you hear . . . ?"

He met Ian's eyes, and Ian replied, "Music?"

Together, they stood up and wandered a few steps away from Mrs. Lambchop. The noise grew louder as they drew closer!

This part of the subway platform was a little wider. There was just enough room for four drummers, who were starting to warm up.

They were playing on upside-down buckets, not real drums at all, but that didn't matter. The drumbeat was catchy enough to dance to and loud enough to fill the subway station. If he got any closer to it, Stanley would have to cover his ears!

Ian clapped in time with the fast rhythm, and someone else whistled a tune that went with the beat. Stanley swayed until his whole body rippled.

"I hear that some of New York's best music is in the subway station," Ian yelled to Stanley. "Musicians have to enter a contest to play down here!"

Stanley wondered where Ian had heard that.

Stanley wondered if it was true.

At the same time, Stanley stopped wondering when the train was coming.

Other than a light, hot breeze, he didn't notice when it swept into the station, because the noise of the music canceled the noise of the train and the energy of the drums canceled Stanley's excitement about the subway.

Then Stanley heard an electronic voice. It said, "Stand clear of the closing doors, please."

Then Stanley turned and noticed the train. Its doors had opened already . . . and now they were starting to close.

"Oh no!" he exclaimed. He rushed toward the subway doors, pulling Ian behind him. But it was too late.

He could see Marco, Kamala, and Meera—the kids from his lunch table— through the subway windows.

He could also see his family, trying to find him in the crowded subway car.

Soon they would discover that he'd

been left behind.

Stanley would be in trouble for wandering away.

But first he had to find a way to catch up to his mother and father. And he had no idea how to do it!

Photo Ops

Stanley could see the train disappearing through the subway tunnel. He watched until he could no longer see the red light at the end of the last car.

The drummers kept drumming, but Ian wasn't clapping anymore. He just stood there with his mouth hanging open. He couldn't speak, but he didn't need to. Stanley saw some tears shining in Ian's eyes. Ian was scared, and so was Stanley.

Stanley took a deep breath. He remembered what his mother always said. "We have to stay calm," he announced to Ian. At the Statue of Liberty, he had kept climbing stairs until he met his family at the top. What if he kept riding the train? His family could be waiting at the next station.

"I have an idea," Stanley told Ian. "When the next subway arrives, we will get on it. We will ride to the next stop and see if our parents are there."

"Okay." Ian nodded. "That's a good plan." The boys waited on a bench until another subway screeched into the station a few minutes later.

The doors opened, and some passengers streamed out. The subway car was crowded, so the boys didn't get a seat when they entered. They grabbed a silver pole in the middle of the subway car and hung on tight!

When the subway got going, it was really fast. It was like a roller coaster without the hills or loops! Ian let go of the pole for a second and tried to balance without it. He bent his knees and dug his toes into the floor. "I'm surfing!" he told Stanley.

Arthur would love this, Stanley thought. He missed his family already.

The dark of the subway tunnel gave

way to the light
of a station. At
last! Stanley thought.
They'll be here, I just know it. He
hadn't even met Ian's family yet, but he
would recognize them if they had the
same red hair.

There was only one problem. The subway didn't stop!

As it rushed through the station, an announcer said something surprising. "Times Square next stop!"

Stanley's heart sank. He could guess what that meant.

"This train isn't stopping at every station," he told Ian. "So we're not stopping at the one where our families are probably waiting."

"Oh no!" Ian slumped against the silver pole. "What are we supposed to do now?" he asked.

"Well, this train is going to Times Square. Our families are going to Times Square on their tour. Maybe we will see them there," Stanley said. He tried to sound sure of himself.

Ian nodded. "Okay," he replied. "At least they are with a big group. It should be easy to find them."

When the subway finally stopped, the boys hurried out. They followed the other passengers toward an Exit sign and took an escalator up to the street. There were more musicians in the Times Square station, but this time Stanley and Ian walked right past them. Any minute now, they would find Anya and her tour group!

As soon as they stepped into Times Square, though, Stanley realized it would not be easy. The sidewalk was so full of people that it was like a river.

Above the river of people, there were billboards and advertisements as far as Stanley could see. There were huge screens playing movie trailers and other videos. Some were attached to the sides of the buildings, some were sticking out into the street, and some of them were many stories tall!

There were so many that Stanley didn't know where to look. The lights were so bright that Stanley bet it was like daytime here even at night. There were restaurants, theaters, stores, offices, and even a police station in Times Square. Stanley had never seen such a busy place!

Even if his family were right in the middle of Times Square, how would he ever spot them?

Stanley took the camera out of his pocket. He was nervous now, but he would want to remember everything later. He snapped photos of the biggest, the brightest, the fastest-moving place he had ever visited.

Then he made a decision. "We've got to get out of here," Stanley told Ian. This was not a good place to be lost, because it was not a good place to get found!

He grabbed his friend's hand and hauled him through the crowd. Right now, it was very useful to be flat. There were so many people walking that it was hard to move. But Stanley could slip through the small spaces between them, towing Ian behind!

"Excuse me," Stanley said as he brushed by a man who was walking and eating a giant pretzel at the same time. He was close enough to take a bite (but he didn't).

"Pardon me," Stanley said as he moved past a woman who had dropped a bag in the middle of the sidewalk. He would stop to help, but he was afraid that if he bent down, his flatness would make him blend into the sidewalk. And he did not want anyone to step on him.

Stanley saw a group of kids on the sidewalk. For a minute, he thought they were the kids from the UN, but soon he could see they were not. These kids were wearing matching jackets, like they were on a tour of their own, or maybe a team. They had their cameras out, just like Stanley. But they were not taking pictures of neon signs or tall buildings. They were taking pictures of themselves with some famous characters from a TV show!

"Look!" said Ian. "Kit the Cat!" Even in Scotland, people watched *Jet Pets*.

It was not actually Kit the Cat, but someone dressed in a costume to look just like her. She wore a striped dress and a black hat.

The kids got close for their pictures,

and Kit the Cat wrapped her paw around their shoulders. When the photo was done, she gave each of them a fuzzy high five. Then she posed with more of her fans.

Stanley wasn't sure why there were TV characters in the middle of Times Square. He didn't want his photo taken with Kit the Cat—he had not watched *Jet Pets* since he was little. He just kept walking, watching a big video screen high above Kit's head.

Then he noticed something. Photos of Kit were being shown on that screen!

Stanley stopped in the river of people. He watched again, just to make sure.

On the sidewalk, a girl in a purple sweater smiled next to Kit. Kit the Cat waved and gave her a high five. A few seconds later, Stanley could see their picture on the big screen.

Anyone who was watching could see

it. And a lot of people would be watching! Including—maybe—Mr. and Mrs. Lambchop and Arthur.

"I have a great idea!" Stanley said. He handed his camera to Ian. "Will you take a few pictures of me?" He had a feeling the other kids—and other cameras—would follow.

Ian shrugged. "Okay, sure," he said. He took photos from a couple of different angles.

It did not take long for a crowd to gather. "Look, it's Flat Stanley!" someone called out.

"I have to get his picture!" someone else replied.

Pretty soon, Flat Stanley had just as

many admirers as Kit the Cat!

Ian directed them to stand in line and take turns snapping photos.

Stanley stood sideways so people could see his flatness. He rolled himself up like a poster. He lay on the ground like a rug. Anything to keep the cameras going! For once, Stanley was glad to be world-famous. Right now, he did not want to fit in!

He had figured something out. While people were taking photos of him, a hidden camera was taking pictures of its own. Those were the pictures that were shown high above the crowd.

Stanley made sure he was smiling in all of them. He waved at his fans. He acted like he was having the best day of his life. If his parents were watching, he did not want them to worry. And if he stayed here a little longer, they might even figure out where he was!

Helping Hands

After a while, the fans turned away from Flat Stanley. Another famous TV character had arrived, and now people wanted pictures with him. The crowd stepped away from Ian and Stanley, giving them a little space to breathe.

Any minute now, Stanley thought, my parents will find us right here.

Even in the middle of the New York

crowd, he could hear Ian's stomach grumble.

"I wish I had eaten more noodles," said Ian. "I'm getting hungry!"

There were plenty of places to eat in Times Square. But neither of the boys had money to buy food. "My parents will get you something," Stanley promised. "Just as soon as they find us."

They waited a little longer, but there still was no sign of the Lambchops.

Stanley sighed. "I think we need to go to Plan B," he said.

"What's that?" Ian asked.

"Ask for help if you need it," Stanley said. He was glad his parents had told him this so many times. "And we definitely need it!"

"Who will we ask, though?" said Ian.

"That's the problem," Stanley said. "We're not supposed to talk to strangers. And Times Square is full of strangers."

"Except Kit the Cat," Ian pointed out. "Maybe she will be able to help us?"

Stanley smiled, remembering his favorite part of the old show. "Maybe we could fly away with the Jet Pets!"

Ian leaped into the air, pretending to take off from the Times Square sidewalk.

If we weren't lost in New York, Stanley thought, I'd be having a great time with Ian. He knows how to make me laugh.

But their situation was not something to laugh about. They could not keep waiting in Times Square forever. They needed a grown-up to help.

Stanley looked at the theaters and the lights and the video screens and the traffic.

Ian looked in the opposite direction. He pointed to the police station right in the middle of Times Square, beneath a giant billboard and across from a fast-food restaurant. "The police!" he said. "Maybe they can help us."

Stanley was not so sure. "I thought you went to the police if you were in trouble. Not if you were trying to get out of trouble." Maybe it was different

in Scotland.

Ian shook his head. "I think they do both things," he said. "It can't hurt to try, right?"

"I guess," Stanley said, still not sure. The police in movies caught robbers and carried handcuffs. They had the occasional car chase. They did not spend much time with kids.

And there was another problem, too. How were they ever going to get there? Two lanes of New York City traffic separated the boys from the police station. Stanley was not used to crossing streets by himself.

Ian covered his ears as a fire truck raced by, sirens blaring. Stanley took a step back as a double-decker tour bus sped around a corner. It seemed like the cars would never stop.

When the light turned red, though, Times Square was quiet for a moment.

"Too bad there isn't a crossing guard!" said Ian. "But we've got this."

He waited for the Walk sign to light up at the crosswalk, then hurried across before the light could change back. "Stanley, come on!" he called over his shoulder.

Stanley took a deep breath and stepped off the curb. He wasn't used to doing this alone. But he wasn't used to being lost in the middle of New York without any adults, either.

"Phew!" said Stanley when they were safely on the other side. "We made it!"

Ian was brave to go first, thought Stanley. Now it's my turn to be brave.

Before he could lose his nerve, Stanley marched up to the door of the police station and knocked.

A police officer came to the door. His name tag said Officer Chapman.  He folded his arms and looked down, frowning. "How may I help you?" he asked. His voice was deep and gruff.

Stanley struggled to get some words out. "We're . . . we're . . ." he stammered.

Ian finished his sentence. "We're lost," he told Officer Chapman. "Can you help us find our families? They are on a tour with a guide from the UN."

Officer Chapman turned to look at

Stanley. His eyes grew large and Stanley saw a smile peek out from under his mustache.

"You must be Stanley Lambchop," he said. "Your parents are looking everywhere for you!"

Anya Petersen had brought their parents into the station, Officer Chapman went on to explain. She had told him every stop her tour would be taking. "If you'll excuse me for a moment, I'll just make a few calls," said the police officer. "I should be able to locate them in no time." They had continued the tour once they knew the police were on the case.

While Officer Chapman got on the

phone, Stanley and Ian waited on a long bench. Stanley took out his camera and snapped a few more pictures.

Wait until Arthur sees these, he thought. He's never been inside a police station—especially in New York!

"Can I see?" said Ian, scooting along the bench to get a little closer.

Stanley put the camera between them and reviewed all the photos he had taken so far. The Statue of Liberty, the UN, Grand Central, the subway, Times Square. He had seen a lot of New York, even though he had missed some of the official tour!

The Times Square pictures were pretty cool, he had to admit. On the screen of his camera, Stanley could see the real-life screens in the square. In his pictures, they were stopped in time.

"Wait a minute!" said Ian. "Look at that."

Stanley pushed a button and returned to a photo he had just passed. It showed the big screen where they had seen Kit the Cat—but before Stanley and Ian arrived. Kit was clapping her paws in delight.

Ian pointed at the picture. "Look!" he said again. "Aren't those the kids we met at lunch?" Sure enough, Marco and Kamala and Meera were on-screen near Kit. Rather than posing for pictures, though, they were looking away from her, into the crowd.

"I think they're looking for us!" Ian said.

Stanley scrolled back through a few more pictures to confirm it. The adults and the kids from their UN tour were all stationed along the sidewalk in Times Square. It looked like they had formed a search party!

It was easy to feel small in New York, thought Stanley. It was so big and so busy. Even a celebrity like him did not get much attention. It was easy to get lost . . . and easy to worry that he had been forgotten. The pictures made him feel much better! Just like Stanley and Ian, the tour group was trying hard to get everyone back together.

Stanley half remembered an old song about New York. He did not know all the words, but one of the lines was "If you can make it there, you'll make it anywhere!"

Stanley and Ian had made it through Times Square. Getting lost in New York was a big test, and they had passed! Now, though, Stanley was ready to get back to the tour, to his family, and eventually to the UN.

Empire State Building

When Officer Chapman came back, he was smiling. "Your tour group just arrived at the Empire State Building," he told the boys. "They will be waiting for you there! How about I give you a ride?"

The officer pulled his car up outside the station, and the boys climbed in. The officer did not put his lights or

his siren on, so they could not speed through the traffic. He did show them some sights along the way, though.

He pointed at a sparkly object at the top of a pole on a nearby rooftop. "People come from around the world to watch the ball drop at midnight in Times Square on New Year's Eve," the police officer said. "And that's the ball!"

Stanley had never been allowed to stay up until midnight on New Year's Eve. He had seen pictures of the ball drop, though. At midnight, people threw so much confetti that it looked like there was a snowstorm in Times Square!

At the next light, Officer Chapman stopped by a silver cart with a blue-and-yellow umbrella. "You can't leave New York without visiting a hot dog vendor!" he said. Stanley liked his hot

dog with a thin stripe of ketchup on top, but Ian got his piled with mustard and sauerkraut, just like the police officer. They arrived at the Empire State Building as Stanley swallowed his last delicious bite.

Officer Chapman parked his car and led the boys into the lobby. He spoke with a woman at the front desk, then showed them to the elevator. "Your families are waiting on the Observation Deck," he said. "That is on the eighty-sixth floor!" As he pressed the button to call the elevator, he added, "Enjoy the rest of your trip, Flat Stanley."

"Thank you for rescuing us!" said Stanley.

He could not wait to see his family and tell them about his adventure in New York. As the elevator doors shut, Stanley closed his eyes. He was ready to be whisked to the very top of this skyscraper. What if we are above the clouds? he wondered. Will we be able to see anything?

Two seconds later, the elevator door opened. Stanley and Ian were on a different floor, but it was not the Observation Deck. On the wall in front of them, Stanley saw a sign that said, Tickets This Way.

"I don't think we have any tickets," Ian said.

A woman in the elevator overheard

him. "That's okay," she said. "You can get your tickets here. Then you take a different elevator to the deck."

The line for tickets wove back and forth across a large room. "This is going to take forever!" Ian complained. "What if our parents get tired of waiting?"

But that was not the only problem. When Stanley caught sight of the ticket counter, he realized they would have to pay for tickets—and they didn't have any money.

Stanley blinked. He remembered the rules for getting lost. But he didn't think he could stay calm this time. And who was going to help them now? Why would anyone want to buy two extra tickets for him and Ian? Stanley could see the tickets were expensive.

He turned to Ian to tell him the bad news. Ian had not noticed the ticket prices yet because he was watching something at the window. "That is so cool!" he said to Stanley. "Did you see?"

Outside the window, there was a platform carrying two people. They were wearing hats and safety glasses, and one of them was holding a pail. As Stanley watched, the platform lowered until it disappeared from view.

"They're window washers!" Ian said. "They ride that platform to every floor, like it's an elevator on the outside of the building. Then they wash

the windows by hand."

Stanley blinked again. He did not know how Ian knew this. But it gave him an idea.

Quickly, he explained the situation to his friend. They could not buy tickets, but they had to get to the top of the Empire State Building. Ian should keep their place in line, just in case. Meanwhile, Stanley would try to get to the Observation Deck a different way.

He left the waiting room and got into the elevator, heading down. He walked through the lobby and back to the street. The police officer had already left, but the window washers had just arrived. They climbed off their platform and shook the last drops from their empty pail. "I'll refill the water," one window washer said to the other.

Stanley did not know how long that would take, and he did not stop to find out.

As soon as they stepped away, he hopped onto the platform himself. There was not much room, but Stanley was comfortable when he flattened himself against one side. Then he tucked himself behind a large tarp the window washers used to mop up any extra water. He would be safe here, Stanley thought. And no one would be able to see him.

In no time, the window washers were back with their pail of water. They stepped onto the platform and buckled themselves into safety harnesses. "To the top!" one of them shouted. That must be the signal, Stanley thought. As soon as the words were out of his

mouth, the platform started to rise up
the side of the Empire State Building!

Under the tarp, Stanley's heart raced.
He could not see how high the platform

went, but he felt like it was riding into outer space. Before long, the air grew cold. Stanley could feel the platform bouncing in the wind. He could hear airplanes in the distance, and maybe some seagulls. But he could not hear any traffic from the street now. He had to be really far away, he figured. Maybe thirty stories up? That meant there was still a long way to go. The building had 102 floors!

Part of Stanley wanted to peek out from under the tarp, just to see. Another part of him was afraid of what he would see. He might get dizzy from the great height, he thought. And while his flatness was helping him hide, it was also a danger up here. One stiff breeze, and he would flutter off the platform like a piece of paper.

The water sloshed over the side of the pail, and one of the window washers reached for the tarp.

Stanley shrank away, but the tarp tickled the side of his nose.

Suddenly, without warning, Stanley sneezed.

The window washer jumped away from the tarp, and the whole platform shuddered. When it settled down again, the window washer whisked the tarp away . . . to reveal Stanley.

"We have a stowaway, Bob," he said to the other window washer.

Stanley shivered. What happened to stowaways high above New York? he wondered. He hoped they did not get thrown overboard.

Bob's eyes grew huge. "How did you get here?" he asked. "What do you think you are doing?"

Stanley held on tight to the edge of the platform. He tried to stay away from the angry window washers, but he could not get very far. "I just needed a ride to the Observation Deck," Stanley said, his cheeks growing red. "I could not figure out another way to get there."

Bob scowled. "Most people take the elevator," he said. "They stand in line, they buy a ticket, and they follow the rules."

Pete was a little nicer. "Hey, he's just a kid," he told his partner. "He's come this far already. What's wrong with giving him a lift?"

Bob shook his head in disappointment. "Kids today," he added. "Always trying to see what they can get away with."

Stanley wrapped his arms around himself. Without the tarp, it was freezing up here.

Pete noticed his movement. Then he noticed something else. "Look, Bob, he's not just any kid," he pointed out. "He's a flat kid. I think that's Stanley Lambchop!"

"Is that so?" said Bob. "Well, Stanley Lambchop, do your parents know where you are? I don't think they will be happy to hear what you're up to."

Stanley just had to convince the window washers to take him to the

Observation Deck. He did not have any other ideas!

"That's the whole problem!" he exclaimed. "They don't know where I am at all! I have been in New York City all alone. Well, not alone but with my friend Ian. We have come a long way on our own. All I need is someone to take me to the top."

He used the window washers' signal on purpose. Would it convince Bob to take him up? Or would he have to go back to the lobby and start all over?

Lost and Found

Bob shook his head, but he did not say no. Pete read Bob's expression and spoke for both of them.

"We'll drop you off at the Observation Deck," Pete told Stanley. "But then we have a job to do."

Relieved, Stanley changed the subject. "How long does it take to wash all those windows?" he asked. There had to be thousands of them!

"It can take months to wash the whole building," Pete said. "And then we start all over again!"

It sounded like a hard job. But what an amazing place to work! On a clear day, Pete said, they could see five different states from the top.

Reeled up on long wires, the platform moved more slowly as it finished its journey to the top of the Empire State Building. When the platform was perfectly still, Bob and Pete each grabbed one of Stanley's shoulders and lifted him over a wall. Suddenly Stanley was on the Observation Deck with a crowd of tourists again. It almost felt like being in the middle of Times Square!

"Good-bye! Thanks again!" Stanley waved as Bob and Pete rode their platform back to the lower floors to wash windows. Right away, he started to look for his parents and Arthur, or for Anya Petersen, or for anyone he had met at the UN. Soon, though, Stanley was distracted by the view.

He had wondered if he'd be above the clouds, but right now there were no

clouds at all. He did not need to worry if he could see anything. Actually, he could see everything! Below him were rows and rows of skyscrapers, plus a green rectangle that had to be New York's Central Park. From this height, he could see the glow of Times Square and a ribbon of yellow taxis on a city street. He could see bridges and ferries and the Statue of Liberty far in the distance, a tiny green speck on an island, with a twinkle at the end of her torch.

The Observation Deck wrapped all the way around the top of the Empire State Building, so Stanley could see the city from every direction. A map on the wall showed him how to locate

Brooklyn in one direction, and New Jersey in another. At the edge of his vision, he wondered if he could see the Atlantic Ocean.

Stanley waited to use some high-powered binoculars that were attached to the edge of the deck. If he focused carefully, he wondered, could he see his hotel? When it was his turn, he realized he needed to drop a quarter in the slot to make them work. Stanley stepped away from the binoculars and rummaged in his pockets to see if he had just one coin. The next person in line stepped forward and tapped him on the shoulder.

"I think you dropped this," a voice

said, handing Stanley a quarter. When Stanley looked up, he saw that it was Ian! "You made it!" Stanley said.

"Bob and Pete found me in the lobby and bought me a ticket," Ian said. "They said they were worried about me and wanted me to find you. They were so nice! Well, Pete especially was."

If they keep helping kids, Stanley thought, they will never get the windows washed! But he was glad they had delivered his friend. He slipped the quarter into the binoculars, and he and Ian each looked through one of the eyes. "I see the UN!" said Stanley.

"I see the moon!" said Ian.

"I see the sun!" Stanley retorted.

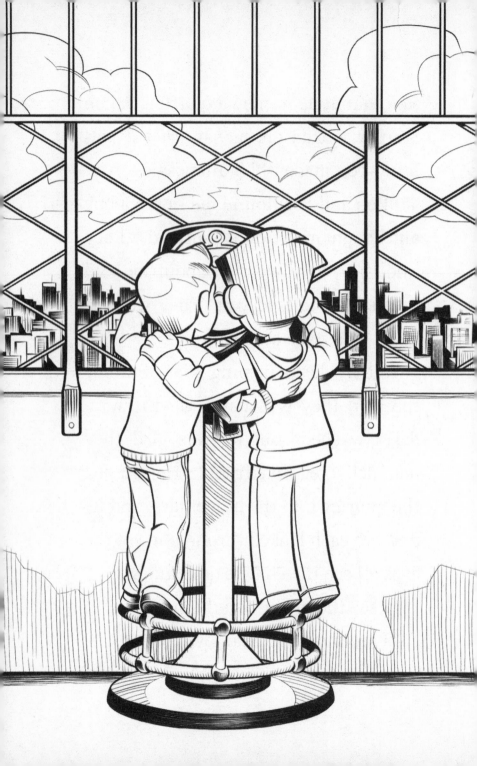

"I see Mars!" said Ian.

That can't be true, thought Stanley. But he said, "Oh yeah? I see Jupiter!"

They were all the way up to Pluto when Stanley decided to turn the binoculars in a different direction. Next thing he knew, he was looking at a familiar face in extra close-up. "Arthur!" Stanley shouted happily.

"I found them!" Arthur called out to Mr. and Mrs. Lambchop.

They rushed over to hug Stanley and Ian. "We're so glad you're safe!" they said. "Don't ever wander away again!"

When the boys told their whole story, the Lambchops were proud to hear how they had found their way back to the tour with a little help, some smart ideas, and some good luck. "I want to see your pictures!" said Arthur. "And I can't believe you met Kit the Cat!"

Anya Petersen arrived with Ian's parents, and the boys told the story all over again. Then Marco and Kamala and Meera showed up. "Look what we got at the gift shop!" Meera said. All at once, the three kids put something on their heads. Each one had a brand-new Statue of Liberty crown! "So we can all match," said Kamala. "No matter where we're from."

Even though he'd been lost in New York, Stanley thought, he had found something important. He had found

some new friends, just like he'd hoped!
Ian was hilarious and full of good
ideas. The others barely knew him yet,
but they'd searched the city streets for
Stanley and Ian because they cared.
And Stanley had made some other

friends along the way, too, from the police officer to Bob and Pete and even Kit. I'm ready to sign the Declaration of Friendship, Stanley thought. And New York is the perfect place to do it! This city brings people together.

Anya Petersen led the group back to the UN, and Stanley was careful not to leave his parents' side. When there was music in the subway, he just sang along under his breath. When Ian tried to surf again, Stanley stayed in his seat. But when they returned to the UN, Stanley hung back. As the rest of the group entered UN territory, Stanley waited one more second in New York.

He wanted his visit to last as long as possible! And then he went to pledge his friendship to the other kids, for now and for the future.

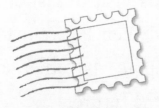

WHAT YOU NEED TO KNOW ABOUT NEW YORK CITY!

There are currently 472 subway stations in New York City, served by 25 subway lines. In 2016, over 5 million people rode the New York City subway each day, and more than 1.5 billion people ride the subway each year.

When the Brooklyn Bridge opened in 1883, it was the longest suspension bridge in the world at 1,595 feet long (486 meters).

When the Statue of Liberty was last restored, in 1986, the torch was covered in sheets of twenty-four karat gold.

No one knows exactly how many rats there are in New York City. The best estimate is around two million, or about one rat for every four humans.

New Yorkers come from all over the world. About one half of all New Yorkers speak a different language than English.

New York City is an archipelago, or a group of islands. Four out of the city's five boroughs are an island or are connected to an island (Manhattan Island, Staten Island, and Long Island, which includes Queens and Brooklyn). The Bronx is the only borough connected to the mainland United States.

The original inhabitants of Manhattan were Native Americans called the Lenape. Lenape means "the people" in the Native language Munsee. They called this territory "Manahatta," meaning "hilly island."

Times Square used to be called Longacre Square, until 1904 when the New York Times headquarters moved to the neighborhood.

There are around 3,000 food carts in New York City, and the most popular item they sell is coffee.